Grogbottom's Favourite Drink

Jamie Wilson

PublishAmerica
Baltimore

© 2010 by Jamie Wilson.
All rights reserved. No part of this book may be reproduced, stored in a retrieval system or transmitted in any form or by any means without the prior written permission of the publishers, except by a reviewer who may quote brief passages in a review to be printed in a newspaper, magazine or journal.

First printing

All characters in this book are fictitious, and any resemblance to real persons, living or dead, is coincidental.

PublishAmerica has allowed this work to remain exactly as the author intended, verbatim, without editorial input.

ISBN: 978-1-4489-7627-0
PUBLISHED BY PUBLISHAMERICA, LLLP
www.publishamerica.com
Baltimore

Printed in the United States of America

Foreword
Eugene Digory Pipkins & Captain Grogbottom

Captain Grogbottom. Born in Henley-On-Thames in 1793 to a middle-class family, Eugene Digory Pipkins was the son of the Prussian Lord Helrich Von Gurschlesten and Lady Anna Pipkins of Hartford Manor. Eugene was born with a full beard and hair on his chest, back and shoulders. Distressed by this somewhat surprising turn, Lord Von Gurschlesten immediately saw fit to blame the problem on his wife and cast rumours about her being hairier than an ape from the neck down. Rather than generate sympathy for himself, the general public thought him a queer sought being as he allowed himself to be married to such a fur-ball in the first place. The whispering that preceded and silence that followed his entrance to any meeting place eventually cast so much embarrassment and shame on him that he attempted to take his life. Unfortunately documented court hearings of the time did not specify exactly how he attempted to end his life but what is clear is that he failed, and at the time suicide was illegal and punished by death. As such Lord Von Gurschlesten was hanged in public in October 1794. Following this unsettled period, the then Lady Von Gurschlesten changed her name back to Pipkins so as to dissociated herself with what had become a rather famous name.

During his formative years and education, Eugene never excelled at anything. His etiquette lessons were disastrous given his inability to use a fork for anything other than slaughtering small animals. He used his hands at the dinner table and had such appalling speech that he was rarely able to make much noise other than "Arrgh" which tended not to make for good first impressions. At 13 years young Pipkins tried his hand at fencing for the first time, but was soundly beaten while still studying the protective mask by the young French squire Sabastien Le Plonq. So enraged was Eugene that he picked up the nearest thing he could find, which happened to be the son of Earl Robinson of Hook, and swung him wildly around, knocking down the French squire thus earning himself a reputation as a bit of loose cannon. Determined not to give up on her son, Lady Pipkins put him into the Army for officer training, another ill-fated move which resulted in an entire platoon being killed by an avalanche after Eugene threw a tantrum on top of a rocky cliff face.

The following years saw Eugene and his mother moving around the Home Counties. Slowly but surely, his mother grew steadily tired with his utter inability to engage with people on a normal level and invested less and less time in his formal education. As this happened Eugene found himself hanging around with the naughty boys who feared his large frame and unpredictable nature. Due to this perfectly rational fear, they were willing to do whatever he asked, and as such Eugene accidentally built up an empire on the streets of Stratford that caused mischief at just about every conceivable moment. One thing lead to another and by the time he was 23 Eugene Digory Pipkins had acquired the name Grogbottom (due to an unexplainable poor taste in rum) and the self-appointed title of Captain. He had also taken to piracy like a duck to water, enjoying tax-free riches and the freedom of the ocean. Any fights he found himself in afforded him the opportunity to make use of his exceptional sword play, which involved wildly thrashing his cutlass around, more often than not with his eyes shut. Despite a few close brushes with the law he enjoyed this luxury until the age of 54, which is when he met the Gypsy witch Lorabella Diath. Grogbottom took many treasures from her and gave in return a barrel of grog as a peace keeper, which was not well received by Lorabella. So disgusted was she at being offered what she frankly thought poison as compensation for the treasures he took, she uttered a Gypsy curse on him immediately. The curse would see Grogbottom and his crew dwell in the next world of Jidah, to be tormented by the dark lord Mourdath. This would be until someone of the captain's bloodline would find an omen where no other would see it. Once that descendant had established what the omen was, they'd have to battle through this world and the next to get to the mystical island of Nusketh. Ambiguity was one of Lorabella's favourite pastimes

Chapter 1
Our Hero

Which leads us neatly on to our hero Reginald Walls. This isn't a tale of suspense, though there will be hair-raising moments. Nor is it a tale of many twists and turns, it is simply a tale of a slightly peculiar man's adventure. Which is why I don't have any reason not to tell you upfront that Reginald, hereafter known as Reg, is the very ancestor Grogbottom has been waiting for. He is not the direct descendant, he actually hails from Lady Pipkins' sister, who married into a poorer family (always read everything you sign) and had 18 children. One of which (called Cuthbert) was deemed something of an idiot, though if one took the time to get to know him they found he was just a little off centre. He was, against the wishes of the village elders, allowed to breed, and thus a long line of heritage was born, eventually culminating in the conception of the aforementioned Mr Walls in somewhere around the late 1940's.

Now this story is set nowhere in particular, in a place not dissimilar to anywhere else, and works on the basis that there are three levels of existence—this world (home to Reg), the next world (currently home to Grogbottom) and a place in between (as yet undiscovered). That will be covered in more detail at some point though, and for now let us begin with a shop keeper who is observing Reg walking towards to store. The shop keeper is not a particularly pivotal part in this story either, which will also become apparent by the time you've read the next few paragraphs. Forgive me, I'm blabbering. The bell above the door rang as a our hero came in to the small corner shop.

"Which way is it to Frankie's?" he said.

"Hi Reg, what can I get you," replied the shopkeeper with a big friendly smile.

"Frankie's, which way?" Reg repeated.

"Buddy, Frankie's has been closed since 1974. You're going to have to get Sam to cut your hair ok?" Reg looked confused.

"But I get my hair cut at Frankie's," Reg said in a mumbled voice as he studied the counter. The shopkeeper came out from behind the till to put an arm round his troubled customer. A little about the man himself then. Very poorly educated, and the only perception he has of the world is his own, which in itself is fairly unique. Reg has always maintained he has a rich heritage, though he has no evidence to suggest this. It doesn't matter what anyone else might think though, for he knows. Pirates, Reg, believed. Not wreckers please note, Reg didn't know what they were anyway but he objected at the suggestion that his ancestors were anything other than sea-faring scallywags. Destined for greater things he has always said, but at 63 most people would acknowledge he is leaving it a little late. He rarely appears the most mobile chap, but at times will surprise himself. I'm not sure when the best time to mention my final observation of Reg would be, but as this is the beginning, it would appear to be a good time to say it. When Reg gets excited, he acts in a way he deems to be like that of his forefathers. I digress. As said by the man himself, he gets his hair cut at Frankie's.

"Reg," the shopkeeper said, pulling his attention from the desktop, "why don't you want Sam to do your hair?"

"She couldn't even spell the word scissors," Reg said, now looking down at his feet.

"She can Reg, you can't. Don't be mean." The shopkeeper again drew Reg's attention.

"Can I have some cigarettes?" asked Reg.

"No, you don't smoke. Come, I'll take you home," replied the man compassionately.

"No thanks," Reg said, not abruptly but maybe a little nervously. Reg left the shop and stared down the street. He pulled a compass from his breast pocket to check his bearing, which was north by north-east, and headed towards the last remaining light of the sun. As he walked he dodged and jump every crack in the pavement so as to ensure his late mother's back would not be further pained.

His evening's actions are fairly typical of the man—quirky, to some may be even a little odd. He walked back to his home, a house he'd lived in since the age of 8. The people he lived with were of no relation but over time had become his family, and though he was their lodger, they looked on him fondly as well. I never did fully understand their arrangement given his long stay. It matters not.

"Would you like some tea Reg?" said Enid, the most senior member of the household.

"No thank you," Reg said in a hurried voice, "I must get to bed immediately. I have a big day tomorrow."

"What ever are you doing tomorrow Reggie?" Enid asked a little surprised by his frantic pottering.

"I'm going to Nusketh Island," Reg said as he went into the kitchen, packing pots and pans into a backpack.

"What, where? Nusketh? What on earth for? Is that even a place?" Enid continued to quiz Reg getting gradually more confused.

"Blast you woman! I'm going to Nusketh Island because Frankie's has been closed 23 years and that means the treasure my ancestors buried will surface on the beech within days!" Reg said as he trotted back through the house to the cupboard under the stairs. Opening it he found years of storage to rummage in and started pulling out a strange selection of things.

"Reg, what are you talking about?" Enid started to grow a little concerned.

"Do not involve yourself in things you do not understand, I have a date with destiny and I will not fail my forefathers. Excuse me," and Reg heaved his tent out from under the stacked bric-a-brack.

"What are you doing with that?" Enid said, though she had barely finished her sentence when Reg pinched his nose, drew a deep breath and cursed to the heavens under his breath. He did not reply and simply carried on packing for his adventure. Enid eventually concluded that Reg ought to be left to his own devices and went to cook dinner for her family.

The following morning, those who lived in the house with Reg awoke to find their lodger missing with a note on the table.

"Dear friends,

This morning I have left for Nusketh Island. My journey will be long as I travel on foot, but I must complete the task which lies before me. Frankie's closure of 23 years is the signalling from my ancestors, pirates, who stored their treasure on the beech for me to find there. Frankie's is the Oman, the planets are aliened and now is the time, but I must leave now if I'm to succeed. If I should return, we will be rich. I will buy this house, and you will be my lodgers so I can in return the love you have shown me.

Your friend,

Reg x"

"Have you heard of Nusketh?" said Enid. No-one responded, they just shook their heads. "I didn't think Reg knew how to write," Enid spoke with a most confused tone, very slowly, as she read the note to herself a fourth time.

Chapter 2
Adventures in Piracy

About two miles on from that house, Reg walked against the wind at the beginning of his task. His trousers were rolled up to his knees, he was wearing white socks pulled up over his ankles and open toe sandals. He had a cutlass at his side with a three-quarter length high collared coat over his white silk shirt. A bandanna over his hair, which was covered by a tri-cornered hat completed his attire. On his back he carried a large ruck sack which was maybe 11 years old and had some old brand name inscribed upon it. It carried several pots and pans which were on a string, a tent, a bucket of baked beans and the all important treasure map, which he'd drawn in crayon the night before. Soldiering towards his treasure, Reg was in fine spirit. But the way to Nusketh was perilous indeed, and many tests awaited Reg though he knew not what they would be. The whens, the wheres, all inconsequential. All that mattered was getting there. Reg had a fabulous ethic, indeed he was almost pig-headed, and though the location of Nusketh is not widely known, it was apparently sitting in Reg's mind in the same way you or I might keep the finer points of a school Geography lesson stored. That is to say, it was not immediately at the fore front of his mind, but when he concentrated hard and focused his thoughts, the information was there. Where from this information had come, he did not know; he just knew, somehow.

As our intrepid adventurer approached a dual carriage way in his path, Reg started to head down towards the subway. But when he reached the bottom of the steps, several boys in hoods stood lurking under the road. They whispered to each other, before one stood in front of his friends.

"Gissa fag," said the boy with a look of intent.

"What insolence is this?" said Reg taken aback by the approach.

"You what? You talking to me?" said the boy, fronting up to Reg with his friends close behind.

"Frankie's is shut," said Reg, straightening his back and puffing out his chest. "You what? Gimme your wallet mush," the youth said pulling out a knife.

"A dual? So be it!" and with those words Reg drew the sword from his side, placed his left hand on his hip, scraped his blade across the ground by the boy's feet and struck an en garde. The gang of boys moved round Reg slowly. "I give you this chance to surrender," Reg said looking directly into the ring-leader's eyes.

"Come on 'en!" said the boy as they went all at once. Reg, old though he was, danced out the way. With a smile on his face, Reg knocked the knife from the boy's hand with ease. Another hoody tried to jump on his back but Reg simply ducked. Quickly, two of the boys managed to grab Reg and another ran to hit his face. Reg though threw his legs in the air and kicked the boy down. Then he jumped right back and allowed his weight to topple the lads, breaking his fall with their chests. He jumped back up quickly to be faced by the ring-leader who'd since picked his knife back up.

"Ha ha!!" cried Reg in cavaliering fashion as he again disarmed the boy and cut his tracksuit down the middle, which then fell to the floor leaving the boy standing in just his pants, while the other boys lay in muddled confusion at his feet.

"Hmm, I think that signals victory for me! Bad luck lads," Reg boasted, perching his leg on one of the boys. "Here lad," he said throwing a necklace of sweets to the boy, "Be a good boy and share this your friends." At which he re-sheathed his sword and walked through the subway towards the light. He couldn't stop smiling to himself, a subtle air of confidence, a kind of "I've still got it" feeling which gave him extra spring in his steps. Even if they were just children he thought to himself, even then there were 4 or 5 of them, and he had achieved a most comprehensive victory. His bearing read well on his compass, his map said he was on track, and more than this he knew it in his heart.

As he left the darkness of the subway the sun made him squint, and he took a deep breath of satisfaction. Ahead, only a half a mile or so, there lay a children's park and boating lake. The park was quite large, and given Reg's age he was not able to take on too much on any given day. As such he viewed a small patch on the far side of the large pond by some picnic benches which he thought would make a decent area to pitch up for the night. All that was required for this evening was to cross the lake, so Reg made his way towards the water, looking to commandeer a vessel to take him across the water. Reg approached the boating lake with stealth, hiding behind the small patch of trees to scope the situation. He could see the ideal target in a family of four peddling in their yellow float, having a jolly time. The adrenaline started to flow, the excitement grew. Reg simply loved adventure.

"Hmm," Reg said quietly to himself. "No cannons, not much crew, two cabin boys yet no cabin, no-one visibly armed." Reg scoured the earth for rocks and picked up several large stones which he put into his pockets. Slowly then, he edged forward, tearing off a piece of bush to keep over his head. All around people stared at Reg as he crawled through the park holding half a bush over himself as camouflage. In typical English fashion though, no-one said anything to him, opting instead to mutter disapprovingly under their breath. As he reached the water he threw his cover and started launching stones at the family. A couple of shots skimmed across the bow, another hit the stern but all missed the family.

"Hey," one on-looker, "What the hell are you doing?" The man ran over to try and restrain this strange chap as he continued to hurl rocks at the family. He grabbed Reg as he tried to throw another stone, holding back his arm.

"Ah Har!!" said Reg in fine voice, and pulled his sword once again, pointing it at the man.

"Shit!" said the stranger, leaping back from the crazy old man. He eased back slowly from Reg, and as he did people from all round the park moved forwards towards the scene. Reg put his blade between his teeth and jumped into the water. Everyone stood in amazement as he waded towards the family. The mother and father on the pedalo held their boys close, not sure what to do as Reg got closer. He got to the pedalo and climbed on board.

"Ah Har!" he bellowed once more, clambering onto the yellow pedalo. The family stood horrified by the invasion. "Me name's Reg, and I am commandeering this 'ere vessel. Into the water with you else you'll be'a walkin' the plank!" The family looked into the water, and the father bravely raised his head to Reg.

"There's no plank you idiot, the water's only waist deep!" But Reg waived his sword at him.

"I don't care! Off m' boat you scavanous dogs!" Reg shouted. The dad slipped into the water, and the mother passed one of their children onto his shoulders.

"Brave lads," Reg said as he waited patiently for them to vacate his boat.

"Don't talk to my boys you villain!" The mother said.

"Ooh, feisty gal, I can see why you like her," Reg said to the father, who didn't reply. The mother then got into the water, and the second son climbed onto her shoulders. "Right, I best be going!" Reg said as soon as they were all in the lake, and at that he started to paddle to the other side, about 100 metres away. As he peddled he consulted his map and traced his finger along the yellow line he'd drawn to represent the train line. By his calculations, he'd have a 3 or 4 mile hike on the other side before he'd reach the next stage of his journey. The sun was starting to sink, and as Reg relaxed in his ocean, he began dreaming of pirates, grog and gypsy curses.

Chapter 3
The Rookie

The next morning Reg woke early, maybe 5am. He got up and stretched his legs in the chilly early spring, the dew had not yet lifted and a thin layer of water covered all the benches in the area he'd pitched his tent. Reg was wearing only a pair of y-fronts and his 3 cornered hat, but sat down on the damp bench to take in the morning's air and think about the challenges that lay in wait. After 10 minutes or so he got up and went back into his canvas home to dress and pack.

Within half an hour Reg was just about ready to move. His last action before resuming his travels was to have a bowl of cold baked beans for breakfast. As he sat, labouring his way through the meal, a police car pulled up in the car park of the boating lake. Reg paid no attention, but the officer climbed out of the car and walked up to the picnic area. When Reg eventually did turn round, he saw the uniformed man standing over him.

"Good morning officer," Reg said, not standing or putting his beans aside.

"Good morning sir," the policeman said, somewhat surprised as his eyes followed Reg's outfit up and down. "Erm, sir," the policeman began. Reg pricked up his ears, eased his shoulders back and put his copper bowl of beans on the bench.

"Officer?" Reg replied confidently.

"We had reports yesterday of a..." The policeman stumbled in his delivery.

"Yes come on," Reg said a little impatiently.

"Of an elderly man dressed as a pirate who commandeered a pedalo from a family of of four by throwing stones at them before making them wade through the lake. The man was carrying a sword and was later seen setting up camp in the picnic area where upon he lit a fire and cooked some beans." Reg looked at the ground where the grass was burnt and then to his packed tent and cutlass. "I see," Reg said calmly. "Any idea where this chap might be?" Reg looked the officer in the eye.

"Well, there is…one suspect, yes," the policeman said uneasily.

"Well why are you wasting your time here my lad, get after him!" Reg exclaimed in his wonderfully animated actions. The policeman looked at Reg once more, at his feet by the pile of ash, at the sword by his side and then at his 3 cornered hat. He half laughed nervously and began to walk away before his sense of duty prompted him to stop.

"Ah hah," the officer again nervously laughed, "I think…um, sir I need to place you under arrest."

"Whatever for?" Reg said, quite taken aback.

"Sir, you are the individual responsible," the policeman said.

"Nonsense, you have no proof," Reg said incensed, "I'll not go anywhere with you Mr Policeman."

"Proof? Sir, you are carrying a sword, have a tent packed and there's burnt grass where your standing," the officer said gaining more confidence. "If you don't come with me passively I'll have to hand cuff you." The police officer stood resolutely.

"Will you indeed?" said Reg, his left hand reaching back to the bowl. "Not on your Nelly!" Reg shouted as he threw a handful of baked beans into the policeman's face. The officer yelped as he tried to clean the tomato sauce from his eyes, which had also splattered onto his uniform. Reg put his bag on his back and started running, albeit slowly. Reg had never been a fast runner, and his age in combination with the weight of his back pack meant he was going barely faster than average walking pace. He trotted up the grass bank and through the car park. The policeman behind him had just cleared his eyes from all the juice and started walking after him.

"Oi," he shouted. "Where do you think you're going old man?" Reg didn't turn round but carried on his painfully slow run for freedom. The policeman jogged up to him within a few seconds. He put his hand on Reg's shoulder to turn the fugitive around, but Reg jumped back and drew his sword.

"Are you mad?" the policeman said.

"Maybe a little officer, maybe," Reg replied. The policeman moved his hand slowly round to his belt, reaching for his mace.

"What is it you are doing?" the officer asked with his hand now firmly planted on the spray.

"Absolutely of no interest to you, you young scallywag. I must go now and I don't believe you are trustworthy. As such I shall require you to hand me your cuffs and allow me to go and pursue my gold," Reg pressed his sword against the copper's uniform.

"Ok, here you go," the policeman said very carefully, before suddenly pulling the mace from his belt and spraying it at Reg. Reg was knocked back and the officer ran into him, shoulder-barging into his stomach and knocking him flat on his back. He threw the sword from arms reach and rolled Reg over, kneeling on his back as he put him into hand cuffs. The pain in Reg's eyes was so great that had no idea what was going on, he could only concentrate on the intense stinging. Reg, not being a man of great endurance, soon passed out from the stress. When he awoke, the cloudy vision he had was accompanied by sore wrists, and as he regained his senses he realised that he was in the back of a car. In front, the policeman was driving and talking on his radio. A set back Reg considered, and nothing more. Reg always has a plan, and he would be exercising the rite just as soon as he felt the car journey wasn't going his direction.

The police car pulled up at the station a little while later. The young PC looked in the mirror where he had been checking Reg throughout the journey, which he had spent sleeping fro the most part. However, when he looked now Reg, to the astonishment of the policeman, was not there. Swinging round as if not trusting his mirror the officer gawped at the back seat in search of some kind of answer, but still Reg was not there, and no matter how hard he stared that wouldn't change. With his mouth hanging open, he got out his car and ran back to the end of the road to see if there was any sign of the old man, but he could not see him anywhere. His mouth still open, he traipsed back to his panda car slowly and slung himself down in the front. Thoughts swimming round his head—how? When? How? How? When? The thought "how" was the one mainly in his mind, but the "when" question was just as perplexing. The young police officer sat in his car for several hours before the sunlight drained and he was found, still open-mouthed staring at his windscreen, by one of his colleagues who took him inside for a cup of tea and a session with the police psychiatrist.

But, allow us to wind back to a few hours to when Reg escaped from the police car. Actually no, let us go back to just after he escaped. Some things are after all, best left to the imagination. Had the young PC actually taken a right turn when he ran to the end of the road, he'd have found Reg walking like a man without a care in the world—his chest puffed out and whistling a tuneless drone as he walked. So there it was, he marched triumphantly down towards the bridge over the estuary at the south of the city. Reg wasn't at all sure what city he was in, but he still followed his map and it had led him well so far. In consulting it once more, he ran his finger along the line that led to the island. This bridge was followed a large park area. At the end of the park he needed to cross a motorway, and then over a lake to the island which was situated in the middle, a small raised area with a little vegetation and wildlife.

Chapter 4
Lestigona

As Reg wandered through the city towards the bridge he saw looming in the distance, it occurred to him that he may be lost. He had been walking towards it for some time, but could not seem to get close to it. Through the markets, he'd twice arrived at a point directly underneath, but he simply couldn't find his way to the beginning of the road that led over the water. As he walked through an alley he'd been past at least twice before, a homeless tramp skulked from out of the shadows. "Do you have any spare change for an old man?" the tramp said with his hand outstretched.

"I am not a man for charity, though bartering is occasionally of some interest Tramp. What will I get for my change?" Reg looked the man up and down, and it was a scraggy sight he was confronted by.

"Nothing really," the tramp replied.

"Then you are of no use to me," Reg said abruptly. He turned to be on his way when the tramp held back his shoulder.

"Well I mean, what do you want?" the homeless man said desperately. Reg pondered this for a moment. He didn't really have much to trade, but he had an abundance of baked beans, and the tramp looked like he could use feeding.

"I will feed you, if you will but tell me the way to the bridge" The tramp looked at Reg with fear in his eyes as though Reg had told him of some great evil. "Do you know the way?" Reg said with sincerity.

"Yes," The man said, ageing a year with his answer.

"And will you take me there?"

"Yes, but," and at this the tramp put his hand to his mouth. "The way is perilous, much danger will become us. I will take you, but you must not cross the bridge." Reg stood back from him a moment. He had to cross the bridge, there was no other option. The danger that the old tramp spoke was indeed most disconcerting, but he had little choice other than to face this somewhat ambiguous danger head on. So, Reg made the tramp some beans and had some himself, and then they set off on their road.

It was almost nightfall when they came to the bypass that led onto the road across the bridge. The tramp stopped dead in his tracks. "I will go no further," he said with a sorrowful look. "I implore you, please do not go, it is too dangerous!"

"I must, for it is my journey," said Reg. "Thank you for leading me this far, but you must now stand aside." Reg walked round the tramp and took his first step onto the road. As he did however, a lorry came passed from out of nowhere at a fast speed. It sounded its horn, and thanks to the tramp pulling Reg back, he was able to escape the pull of the vehicle.

"Reg, please do not go that way, it will be the end of you!" said the tramp with all his heart.

"I must," Reg said, "I have to cross the bridge!"

"But you can! Not this way though, there is no path, the cars never stop and the lights are dim! There is another way, a secret way!"

"What?" Reg exclaimed, turning on the tramp. "Why have you not spoken of this before?"

"Because you did not ask," the tramp said pathetically, "You asked me to take you to the road leading to the bridge which I have done. Please, there really is another way!" If you are thinking about a certain novel, you would not be wholly mistaken. Though the tramp didn't have such an "ill-favoured look" about him as another character may have done, he was genuine in his attempt to divert Reg away from danger. Being homeless can often lead to a heightened sense of green-cross-code, learnt in school but perfected on the streets. However, it should be noted that the similarities to this other novel are irrelevant, because that is a work of fiction, whereas Reg's story is not.

"This way you speak of, tell me about it!" Reg spoke angrily as though the tramp had intentionally deceived him. The tramp took a step back.

"There is a secret tunnel, and then…" and this, the tramp whispered in a sinister tone, "There is the stairway." Reg felt uneasy at the prospects, especially at the ill-tone in which they had been presented. But, he had to concede that the journey was suicide if he took the road, and with grave thoughts creeping into his mind, he followed the tramp down another, darker path. They hadn't gone far before their camp was set up, the only nicely grassed area was by a flower bed in the middle of a large roundabout. Reg again shared some beans with his shady companion before they eventually settled down to rest for the night.

The following morning they woke to the sound of traffic—horns and sirens making up the noise of morning rush hour. Reg stood up from his tent to greet the morning in his hat and pants as he always did, much the the dismay of the grid-locked motorists. Sitting down in the chilly morning breeze, he set about lighting a fire to cook breakfast. This of course consisted of beans. He was beginning to get used to his new companion and was about to offer him a bowl when he heard a voice calling from the road. When he looked it was to see the policeman who arrested him, no more than 50 feet away in the road.

"Tramp! Tramp get up!" Reg called in a panic. He threw on his clothes and tore down his tent.

"What's the problem?" the tramp said.

"We are going, now!" Reg said as the last of his remaining things were bundled in to his backpack. The young officer had seen they were readying themselves to run and actually left his car in the middle of the road so he could pursue on foot. "Which way, which way to the tunnel?" Reg screamed at the tramp, who pointed east. With no further hesitation they ran for freedom.

As they ran off the policeman got confused—he desperately wanted to chase them down, as he would only have to jog at best to catch the fugitives, but he couldn't leave his car unattended in the middle of morning rush hour. He stood outside his car stuck in two minds. Reg and the tramp were getting away, albeit slowly, and the car horns of the drivers round him were starting to sound in annoyance. Eventually, much against his will, the policeman got back into his car and put on his siren to part the traffic. He could still just see them as they went around a corner but the vehicles ahead of him were bumper to bumper and found it hard to make way. Spitting blood to the gods, our young PC got through painfully slowly, and when he managed to round the corner, he again found Reg had got away. Boiling with anger, a grim determination set in, Reg would pay for embarrassing him a second time. Again though, had he looked only a little further, he'd have found Reg down a small ally way with his back to a wall catching his breath. The tramp was with him too, though he was less drained as he spent a lot of time running away from danger, such is the life of hobo.

"Is he gone?" The tramp asked a few minutes later.

"I think so, but he's looking for us." Reg was still panting, bent with his hands on his knees. "Police will be all over the city, is there any other way?"

"It doesn't matter," pondered the tramp.

"What do you mean?" Reg said gravely.

"The tunnel, it is not used by anyone other than those who know." They stood over a large man-hole which had been covered over with weeds and rubbish which the tramp had cleared. He held up the lid and invited Reg down below to a dark and murky path. "My people once used to live under ground, we could navigate our way anywhere and not be seen by a soul." Reg did not like the sound of that. He had been through sewers once when he was much younger and didn't much care to repeat the experience. But, with little choice, he followed the tramp down into the murk. Another hour passed and the two men who were becoming to regard themselves as comrades, were walking through the sewers under the streets where a disgruntled policeman hunted them.

"It smells pretty bad down here Tramp," Reg said as they trudged through the dark tunnels. There was some head room as neither men were particularly large in frame.

"Are we going the right way?" asked the tramp. Reg turned round and looked at him, straining his eyes in the dim light.

"What do you mean, I'm following you!"

"This isn't the tunnel, simply a tunnel, which will take us safely through to where we need to go," the tramp said. "It has been many years since I last took this walk." Reg, having decided keeping calm would be the best option, sat himself down against the wall and waited for a trigger in the tramps memory.

"What is your name?" Reg asked his new friend, who was not without mystery.

"My name? Ha!" laughed the tramp quietly to himself. "I'm afraid I don't remember. It has been so long since anyone used it. It is of no matter in any case, call me what you will. Tramp, it would seem, is as good a name as any." Tramp grinned at Reg, who in turn grinned back. There they sat together for some hours to come, and as they sat they talked and told each other stories of their lives. The stories they told were all interesting and perhaps would have a place in a text of their own some day. But alas, there is not space enough to include them into this tale, and so we shall pick up with them as Tramp remembered which way they were supposed to be going, or at least was ready to make an educated guess.

As they moved off in what Tramp thought was the right direction a noise could be heard in the distance which was most terrible. Reg's heart skipped a beat as he turned to look at Tramp who in turn was frozen to the spot. With cold chill in his voice Tramp turned to Reg.

"What was that?" breathed Reg as he unsheathed his cutlass.

"That is...the sound of...the Lestigona," Tramp was barely able to speak, so laced with terror he was. Slowly Reg edged forward towards the sound, gripping his sword with Tramp just behind. Then the noise shrilled through the damp air, much like a gurgling scream you could associate with phlegm-throated baby. It was such a sound that it took all the confidence they had to move on into the blackness. They could barely see more than a metre in front and could only take small steps. Then the sound of pattering feet reverberated around the tunnel. The sound swam round their heads as it echoed, making it feel as though it were all around them. With his blade raised, Reg edged forward again but suddenly felt the skim of some clammy flesh brush past the back of his neck. He spun round, dumb-struck with fear, but only Tramp was behind him.

"Did you see it?" Reg whispered, but Tramp couldn't focus his eyes on Reg. Transfixed, he just managed the smallest of nods. His eyes wide open, his leg started to tremble and the smell of something unpleasant wafted up from the floor. Tramp couldn't move, he just stood trembling, fear had taken him, shell-shocked, paralysed to the spot. Then the noise again, the gargling sound. Loud this time, so close but still they couldn't see it. The pattering footsteps again, they felt the wind of it as it ran behind them. Reg spun round again, breathing so fast he was struggling to keep his wits about him. Suddenly then, a smell rouse quite unlike anything Reg had ever smelt before, though it awakened a memory in Tramp from somewhere deep in the past, not spoken of, blotted out. A smell that would have any normal man faint, were they not already surrounded by the stench of the sewers and a tramp's urine. It was with out doubt the most horrific odour, and it was right under their noses. Because then, just as they were struggling with sight, smell and fear, the Lestigona reared up in front of them. It was an ugly creature, a deformed cat-like head with no skin but what appeared to be flesh that looked burnt in places. It had four legs but was able on two, using the front legs as arms and maiming with its enormous talons. The creature was black as night, and despite being only a whisker away from the pair, it was only the draft of the creatures breathing that betrayed its position to Reg.

It was in that moment that Reg forgot his fear and found his courage, and as the stench of the Lestigona's breath woke his senses, he swung his cutlass round in front of him with a roar of a lion about to commence battle. The Lestigona was quick though, and sees as well in darkness as you or I would in broad daylight. It could see the blade swinging round Reg's head and quickly moved back out of reach and sight into the darkness. Reg's blade crashed against the wall of the narrow chamber and the noised clanged all the way down the corridor. The gurgling sound then could be heard once more, quietly but very close. Then Reg felt something brush past him and without hesitation swung the sword again, and again swiped through the and hit the opposite wall. Reg concentrated hard, positioning himself as best he could to be ready for the creature however it would come. But it didn't come for Reg, it came for Tramp. For just as Reg had readied himself for its next run, his friend let out a cry. Reg turned quickly to see the claws of the creature coming out of the front of Tramps stomach. The strong arm that ran through the man's body lifted him up. Reg initially was frozen to the spot as Tramp moved through the air. He made no sound, but stared with manically fearful eyes at his stomach, touching the Lestigona's arm as though to check it was really happening. But happening it was, and with no further hesitation Reg charged his sword forwards with stout determination and courage. He sliced at the arm as quick as he might but Reg is slow and old, and before the blade came close the arm had been withdrawn and Tramp fell crumpled on the stone floor, in shock and whimpering with pain. The scuttling sound then, the pattering of footsteps again echoing round, confusing Reg as he desperately tried to listen. Nothing he could hear though, no sound now, no noise, no movement. But the smell, that wretched smell still remained. Close the Lestigona was, but where Reg knew not.

Taking a brief moment in the window between attacks, Reg bent down to tend to his injured comrade. As he did, he waved his blade behind him to be sure nothing lurked, and the blade became wedged in something which produced the most awful noise. Reg immediately turned round to find that his blade had been buried in the heart of the Lestigona, which was silently waiting just behind him. The creature writhed and screamed with its gurgling hellish voice, violently swiping and clawing at what stood ahead. Reg was ducked down and cradling Tramp, knowing full well that luck had been favourable to him on this occasion. The Lestigona could see it's dinner, but with the black blood pouring from its damned heart, the creature soon fell, and before long the stench of its lifeless corpse lay on the ground at the duo's feet, with Reg's cutlass standing up from the beast's chest.

Reg staring at Tramp could see the life draining from his eyes also, and held his hand tightly as he slipped away. "Follow your compass east past the fourth ladder, there you will find your way out and into the tunnel before the stairway," Tramp struggled, before his body went limp, his hands went cold, and Reg lay him to rest where he fell. A single tear trickled down Reg's cheek, but he said nothing. He stood up, put a foot on the Lestigona's head and wrenched out his cutlass. Then, checking his compass, moved off as instructed by Tramp.

Having found his way to the ladder, Reg decided to have a rest to think. How did Tramp know of that creature, the Lestigona he called it. Where had it come from? Strangest of all, why did part of him already know what it was? Lestigona. Saying it over and over in his mind, each time it gained something yet remained nothing more than a distant candlelight. Then his thoughts shifted to Tramp, he'd been a good companion, and Reg was sorry to have lost him. He wished he had time to ask his questions, that Tramp would accompany him further. But he couldn't, and then Reg's attention was lost to the whole reason he left his home—treasure. Such wonderful gold, gleaming emeralds, deep ruby stones, diamonds bigger than your fist, gems, sapphire and more gold after that! His ancestors, they would be beaming down on their legacy as Reg, who'd never even learned to read properly, never left home, never really even made any friends, was edging slowly to glory. He snoozed peacefully as he dreamed of juggling treasure and swimming through a golden sea.

Chapter 5
More Tramps and Noah

When he woke up again, Reg felt a little unbalanced. It had been some hours since he'd seen the sunlight and his eyes were now well accustomed to the lack of light. He ascended the ladder and climbed out through the manhole. He'd barely got his feet when he had to dive out of the way of an oncoming car, because as it turned out, the manhole was in the middle of a dual carriage way. Fortunately, it wasn't too busy and he managed to shuffle himself to the side of the road before coming to any harm. Throwing himself over the barrier, he took a moment to gather himself. The sun was still quite high, but he wasn't sure what time it was. Standing up fully, he turned round to see that Tramp had led him well, for he stood by a subway leading under the road he just escaped. Beyond that, he could see a long staircase up to the bridge. The staircase looked damaged and tricky, parts of it were missing all together. It was a hard climb, and who knows what else he might find on his way. But first, under this subway. Nothing to it, surely.

Down the steps he went to the tunnel. It was quite lengthy, and surprisingly dark. There were a large number of people under the road, but they weren't going from one end to the other, they were just wandering aimlessly, bumping into each other. The flickering lights on the ceiling gave a little light through the eerie dusk. An odd proposal, Reg thought to himself. Looking up, the daylight still shone. Strange that it should be so dark under the bridge. But Reg was no runner and the thought of crossing the road above did not really appeal to him, so cautiously he entered the subway.

"Any spare change?" grunted one of the people almost as soon as Reg walked in. He didn't answer but ignored him and kept walking. Then another, and another asked and still Reg carried on. None of them said anything else, but those that had seen him were following behind. There were so many people down there, and it seemed that they were all homeless and all unable to say anything other than the one sentence. Getting a little concerned, Reg tried to up his pace, which was matched by those who followed.

Then suddenly, one of the homeless men tried to take a bite out of Reg! He moved aside quickly, but the man did manage to get his teeth round Reg's arm. And then suddenly it hit Reg that these men, the walking dead, they were surely the work of the Lestigona. The undead, made so by the creature that eats their insides, leaving a corpse that suffers from excruciating hunger, doomed to walk until their heads be severed. This, somehow Reg knew,like he knew of the Lestigona itself. He couldn't have told you if you asked him, but when it confronted him, he just knew. Like a dream you forgot you remembered from your childhood. Like anything that sits in your subconscious, waiting to be disturbed when required. He also knew they shouldn't be here. Any of them—the Lestigona or its victims. He didn't know where they should be, but he was certain they were in the wrong place. Then survival called.

Reg drew his cutlass once again. Never did he think that he'd be using it again as soon as this, the blood of the Lestigona was still smeared across the steel. Reg flashed his blade this way and that, and as he did heads rolled. It was a long way to the other side, but behind him the undead were driven by the smell of his flesh. Hacking and slashing as well he could Reg waded through the bodies. 3 things crossed his mind as he went about dropping corpses—1. It was very sad indeed that these poor wretches had ended up as they did. 2. It was rather good fun, how many times in your life are you going to be able to wander through a subway slaughtering masses of zombies? 3. He was even doing the damned undead a favour, so everyone's a winner.

He was nearing the halfway point of the tunnel, making surprisingly good progress as he gaily swung his cutlass from side to side. Still, despite that being as it was, Reg was in a positive mood and could see the exit at the other end. Tramp had warned him of the dangers he would face in the tunnel, though perhaps could have been a little less cryptic about. No matter though thought Reg, and looking into a pair of dead eyes, he brutally swung his sword and let another head fall to the floor and roll to the wall.

Reg was starting to think of his treasure again, the glistening jewels and endless wealth, it put a smile across his face as another head was severed. He really was so happy that he started to sing to himself, a most satisfying to swing his blade and decapitate zombies—in time with the music in his mind as he skipped towards the other end of the subway.

Finally, Reg reached the other end of the tunnel. Not nearly as hard or scary as he thought it would be, but then he deserved a break after the incident with the Lestigona. The only slightly odd thing was that the sun was now set and night was upon him, which was strange because he'd been in the tunnel barely 20 minutes. Still, not to worry he thought, and he set himself for the night at the bottom of the stairs, ready for a climb in the morning.

Reg woke after little more than a couple of hours. The sun was still sleeping, and the world still shrouded in darkness. But Reg was wide awake and ready to go, so heaving himself up, he started to climb. Looking up, he could see a mountain of steps before him, it would take some time. Step after step, he ascended slowly but steadily. There were gaps, missing steps, places were he had to drag himself up to the next level. After a couple of hours, he decided to take a short rest. Reg's bucket of beans was starting to get a little low so he helped himself to only a small bowlful just to top him up for the next couple of hours. As he sat down, thinking of course of his treasure, a small bird flew down and landed on the banister.

"Hello little friend," Reg said to the bird. The wagtail chirped back, as though it was answering his greeting. Then Reg noticed a small note attached to its foot. He took it and read it, intrigued by the discovery. It was a note from the wagtail's mum, much to Reg's surprise.

'Whoever finds this letter

My son is on his way back from a mission to the mainland to check our migration route. If you can, please spare him some food on his way back to his home, the island of Nusketh.

My thanks, squawk."

Reg put the letter down from his eyes and looked at the bird again, who chirped as he did. "Well little friend, I too am on my way to Nusketh island, perhaps you'd like to come with me?" The wagtail let out an excitable chirrup and flapped it wings a little. It bought a smile to Reg's face, and he tapped his shoulder, beckoning the little bird to come and perch. Feeling a new sense of enthusiasm, he fed the little wagtail some beans and then started to climb again with his friend on his shoulder.

They climbed together for some time, Reg told the bird his stories, old and new. After a while, Reg decided that the little wagtail ought to have a name, and with the approval of his friend, he called him Noah. Noah was a name that Reg liked very much, and though he'd never read the bible (or any other narrative for that matter) he was pretty sure he'd named after someone important, and he liked that.

Chapter 6
Guardians of the Bridge

After almost 6 hours, they had done about a quarter of the climb. They came to a section where was a small area with a bench and some flowers in a little public display. On the bench sat a man wearing a suit of armour, with a lance, sword and shield. As the man saw Reg and Noah, he got up and stood before them.

"None may pass," the man said holding his shield in front of him and his lance by his side.

"Err…sorry, who are you?" Reg asked a little taken aback.

"I am Krell, and I am the youngest of the Brotherhood, Guardians of the bridge."

"Right," Reg said, scratching his head under his hat. "Well Krell, there were no signs saying private land or anything, I was under the impression that this was council maintained land."

"They carry out the maintenance it's true, the stairway hasn't always been in such a poor state you know. But, that is not our concern. You have come up the secret stairway, only those who know of it can find it. How is it that you came to be in front of me now?" Reg told him of Tramp and showed him the map he had drawn. The colour from the crayon was starting to smudge a little and it was starting to look a bit of a mess. In fact, it is fair to say it didn't look to good to begin with, but now it was a crumpled up scrap of paper with an orange and yellow mess on it. Krell looked at it, looked at Reg, and looked at the map again. "This map has brought you here?" he said. Reg nodded. "And you've never been here before?" To this Reg shook his his head. Krell further studied his map. "Well traveller, I don't understand how you have been following this map, for I can't make out anything more than a brownish smudge. But led you it has, and here you are. But alas, I fear your journey has been in vein for I cannot allow you to pass."

"But why ever not?" Reg asked with bewilderment.

"Oh, well as I said I am the youngest of the Brotherhood, blah, blah, blah, you can't pass," Krell replied with a shrug and a sigh.

"But why?" Reg asked again, more impatiently than before.

"Because you have no business on the other side of the bridge. You are seeking treasures and wealth, not reasons we in the Brotherhood look upon with great sympathy." Krell spoke in a very patronising way which annoyed Reg greatly. "How do you know about the treasure?"

"Same way I know about the Lestigona."

"You know about the Lestigona?"

"There are only two things that need concern you presently, one is that I know all I need to know and the other is that you cannot pass. Clear?" This quickly served to force Reg into losing what little temper he retained.

"Then I challenge you!" Reg said with his chest puffed out and his hand on his sword. Noah chirped as well, clearly supporting Reg in his actions.

"Challenge me? Fine. You done this before?" Krell asked, clearly very bored of the whole thing. Reg shook his head. "Right. The recognised challenge is an ancient sport of combat called Nacrine." Krell took off his steel gauntlets. "I would presume you're not familiar with the rules so listen well for I'm no fan of repetition. You put your hands together like-so," and Krell demonstrated by doing just that. "We then put out our hands so that the tips of or finger are just touching. Now then, I will attempt to slap your hand, and you must try to avoid the blow. If you do, you may attempt to strike my hand. Whoever manages to register 3 consecutive strikes will be victorious." Reg looked him in the eye.

"Slaps?"

"I beg your pardon?" Krell replied.

"Slaps! Slaps, the game your telling me about is slaps. Your game that you play to let people over the bridge, you play slaps?" Reg was amazed that such a children's game would be an 'ancient sport of combat' as the guardian put it. But, at least there was no real pain involved, no risk to long term health or anything. So, accepting his choice of engagement, Reg raised his hands to take on Krell.

Krell we have to remember was the youngest of the Brotherhood, and although we don't know how long he'd been there, it does seem safe to assume he wasn't posted there recently. The youngest brothers in families tend to gain a reputation for being bad losers and this had made him very competitive in nature. They put there hands together, their fingertips just touching. Then Krell swiped, and struck Reg hard. "OW!!" Reg said, surprised at the force behind the slap. Krell smirked as they re-took their positions. They had barely done so when Krell swiped again, harder and faster than the first, and as Reg as reeling he went to give the third and final blow when Reg managed to move his hands out of harms way. "Harr!" growled Reg with an air of confidence. It was Reg's turn. They took their position again, but Reg was slow as ever and Krell who'd played this game many times moved his hands with ease. Krell smiled again, and quickly landed 2 slaps on Reg's hands. Then, faking a third blow made Reg flinch. He did this twice more, making Reg nervous as he winced with every muscle movement in Krell's hand. Then Krell made his play, and Reg just moved his hands enough to feel the air from Krell's slap faintly over the top. Reg then quickly, or as quickly as Reg can manage, slapped out and caught Krell off guard. Reg smiled, Krell frowned. Reg took to looking Krell in the eye, and Krell being a proud man was not shy of such antics, and met his stare with a steely face. Reg then slapped again, and this time got Krell with a direct hit. Reg needed one more. He racked his brain trying desperately to think of a way to distract him when Noah chirped. It wasn't much, but it gave Krell the split second lack of concentration Reg needed and swiftly he took advantage and landed a blow across the back of Krell's hands. Krell then became most angry.

"Damn!" he cried. "Damn you and damn your bird, Aagh!!!" Krell angry roar echoed out over the bridge and into the night sky that surrounded them. Reg turned round and winked at Noah, who chirped back at him. Krell was really very annoyed and huffed back to the bench making a terribly clunking noise with his armour as he walked. Throwing himself back onto the bench he huffed a big sigh, folded his arms, puffed out his cheeks and stewed. Reg carried on up the stairs past Krell who he left, still in a sulk and in no mood to wish Reg well. Noah sat merrily on his shoulder, and they looked up to see another mile of ascent to come.

The hours passed, and Reg, with his new and trusted companion Noah, climbed ever slowly up the steps. It was some hours later when they finally approached what was halfway, though they knew not how far they had come, only that it seemed an endless hike to the top. At this stage they found a similar area to the one where they met Krell, the same bench, flowerbeds and indeed another man. He was dressed in a suit of armour also, and as he saw them he took to his feet to greet them.

"Good evening fine sirs," the man said, offering a handshake to Reg and some seeds to Noah. "What brings you this way?"

"We are travelling to Nusketh gallant knight, and bid we may pass to the top of this stairway." Reg then told him the same tale as he had told Krell, and when the man asked of Krell Reg told him he had won a battle of Nacrine.

"You indeed have my respect, for it takes a fine man to defeat Krell in Nacrine. It is his favourite game and he has not been beaten in many centuries. I expect he was most unhappy to have lost today, yes?" Reg nodded with a small grin. "You smile at your victory, but you know not what you have done." The knight, although polite and friendly, spoke with serious tones in his voice. "My name is Endorinn second in the Brotherhood, Guardians of the bridge, and in order to pass me you must defeat me in battle. If you lose, you must go back down the steps. However, you must defeat Krell again when you get back to that point, and if you do not you will be destined to live, die and rot on this very stairway." Reg, despite being not entirely thrilled at the news, was in good spirits and rather enjoying these little activities. They kept his brain active and it was very exciting to meet these people dressed in suits of armour, he'd never met knights before.

"Endorinn, second in the Brotherhood, name your weapon." Reg spoke with confidence as he put his hand on his cutlass.

"So hasty to draw your sword?" Endorinn said, looking quizzically at Reg.

"Oh, sorry," Reg said, struggling to come to grips with the ways of the Guardians. "So what is my challenge?" Endorinn stepped forward and pulled a small bag from his armour. "Take this," Endorinn said, passing Reg what looked like a straw. Then he pulled out two small boxes open at one end and a ball. "The game is called Zuphir and has been used to settle disputes since ancient times. Use your straw to attempt to blow the ball in my box. If you succeed three times you will be free to pass."

"Are you kidding?" Reg said, struggling not to laugh.

"Do I strike you as someone who likes to joke?" Endorinn replied gravely.

"No, not especially. But I played slaps with Krell, and now you want me to play blow football!" Reg let out a chuckle, because he knew something Endorinn didn't. Reg was the junior national blow football champion for six consecutive years, and though it had been a while, it's not the sort of talent you lose overnight. So, with his cards to his chest Reg knelt down took up his straw. Endorinn was an excellent player of Zuphir, but Reg was a master, and made light work of Endorinn. Three times he'd blown the ball into his box before Endorinn had registered but one. And, as it turns out, Endorinn was no better in defeat than his sulky younger brother, for in a fit of rage he kicked the small boxes down the steps, broke the straws and threw the ball over the side. Then he stamped his feet round in circles, huffing and blowing from his cheeks in a most unsatisfied manner. Noah flew back to Reg's shoulder, and they soldiered on up the steps to whatever lay in wait ahead.

Hours passed, and still the sun did not rise. It had been almost twenty four hours that they'd been on the stairway and daylight hadn't once threatened to shine, and hadn't since before he entered the tunnel. But he grew close to the summit, and it was now in sight. The climb had been a monumental task, like scaling an extremely practical mountain. But scale it they did and they now found themselves in front of a large wrought iron gate in a grand courtyard, defended by a giant of a man. The eldest of the Brotherhood Reg presumed, he stood taller than any many Reg had ever met and struck fear into his stout heart. The final Guardian was called Zuante. He walked forward to Reg as the first man he had seen in an age. Placing his hands on his face, he studied Reg's features like a grandparent whose seen a child for the first time. Then he embraced Reg, much to the old pirates surprise. Reg stood uncomfortably still with Zuante's arms encompassing him.

"Err...hello?" Reg said, his voice muffled as he was hugged up against the giant. Zuante said nothing, but hushed him as he cradled him. Then, an uncomfortable silence ensued for several minutes. Eventually, Zuante let go and Reg stepped back. "Well, this is all a bit awkward isn't it," Reg said. Zuante said nothing, but smiled gently at him.

"It has been many years since I last set eyes on another human. You are most beautiful." Zuante had clearly gone a bit squiffy in his years of solitude.

"Um, ok. Thanks, I think. I need to pass through the gate," Reg stood like a schoolchild in front of a headmaster.

"But whatever for?" Zuante said, his eyes turning to disappointment. Reg told him of his quest and explained that he really wished to be going as soon as possible. "Fine, if you must. You've defeated both my brothers so clearly your very talented. I expect you're starting to understand our ways in respect of passing, your final challenge is a game called Yinear. If you win you pass, if you lose you die, hell fire and eternal damnation, etc., etc. Do you follow so far?" Reg nodded. "Good. The rules then—we both put out a fist, and on the count of three you chose to either make a fist, put up to fingers or have your hand outstretched. The fist..."

"I suspect I know," Reg interrupted. "Clearly your ancient methods of combat are child's play, I know it as Paper, Scissors, Stone. Are you ready?"

"Err...ok. Are you ready?"

"Yes, let's go." Play ensued, and Reg played paper against Zuante's stone. He won, again. He had defeated the 3 Guardians of the bridge, and with a heavy heart Zuante opened the large iron gates. Reg walked through from the marvellous courtyard into glorious sunshine, at the better end of the long bridge. Looking back through to the courtyard night still loomed, yet here he stood just on the other side in broad daylight. "How has this happened?" Reg said with amazement. Zuante smiled back.

"Sometimes good fortune will lead you to a new place, but it was fate that led you to the Tramp, and destiny that he led you to this portal." Still smiling, Zuante starting closing the gates behind Reg.

"Wait, how do you know my name? How do you about Tramp? How is any of this possible?" cried Reg, but with no hope of knowing, for the gates shut and joined seamlessly with the bridge, and when Reg tried to see where it had gone there was nothing there at all. Confused, Reg started to walk down the rest of the road to the end of the bridge. There were no cars any more, there was no wind and Reg couldn't hear anything more than the sound of his own footsteps.

Chapter 7
Keeper of the Realm

A short while later Reg had completed the bridge, and consulting his map, worked out his route through the park. It was really very pretty, the sun shone through the trees in wonderful rays of light. The trees themselves were green and luscious. The temperature was very agreeable—not hot or cold, no breeze, everything was just nice. But somehow, this didn't relax Reg at all. In fact he felt a good deal less comfortable now than he did when he was climbing the stairs. Noah hadn't chirped once since he got to the bridge and things, despite the scenic beauty, didn't feel right at all. But walk on he did, and through the park he saw wonderful sunflowers standing 6 feet tall, daisies and dandelions covering long stretches of the ground either side of the path. There were so many flowers, bright and colourful all around, they were all perfectly kept and presented in beds that were cut and trimmed. The grass was similar in length to that which you might find on a golfing green. The whole park was so well constructed it had to be man-made, but there was no evidence of life anywhere to be seen. Still Reg walked, and for an hour or more his trek through the park went without any noise whatsoever.

Which, as it turned out, he soon missed. For when he eventually was confronted by the power of the land, he found himself in much more of a pickle than he had thought possible. It was just after entering a garden, walled off from the park with a gate for access, most beautiful with separate flower beds and fountains—a garden within a garden if you will. In this space he found a cloaked man with a long beard and a lawnmower. He was not of an intimidating size or appearance, the man's face looked older than his body. He had lines across his head which would have you guess his age to be around 50, but he was strong and worked at his garden with the energy of a man half his age. Although Reg grew closer, the man did not make any eye contact, he ignored Reg's presence completely. That was until Reg was upon him and went to ask a question. At that moment, the man threw his gardening tools to one side and thrust his hand into the air, suspending Reg 3 feet above the ground.

"What? How are you doing this?" Reg cried with fear and confusion.

"What are you doing in my land?" The man shouted back.

"Your land? I didn't know, I seek only a path to Nusketh!"

"Have you walked on the grass?" The man said seriously. "What?"

"HAVE YOU WALKED ON THE GRASS?"

"No, no I haven't—I swear! Please let me down!" Reg was so scared that his voice trembled when he spoke.

"You wreak of fear, how can this be the man that defeated the guardians? Did you trick them?"

"Defeated them?"

"No-one has won Zuphir since Endorinn was a child!" At this, the man let Reg drop to the floor. He walked around him as Reg whimpered, scared and alone.

"You are a poor excuse for a man. This land is my land, and no man has passed into my realm for many an age. What do you seek?" Reg rolled over puffing air and clutching his lower back. The recovery time took a while, and all through the screwing up of his face and pained expressions Gorgain stared in bewilderment at this most peculiar of adventurers. "Are you ok?" he asked eventually, and Reg nodded his head and stretched his back out, clicking a few joints in the process. Gorgain had never enquired into another man's health before, but then all others that had come into his land were somewhat more in conquest and the like. Eventually Gorgain sat down on the grass he talked of moments before to let Reg get his breath back, which took a while longer. And then, after some more time had passed and Reg's blood pressure had returned to something closer to normal, he saw fit to ask a question of his host.

"How did you make me float like that?" A perfectly reasonable question by any standards Reg though.

"Can you not do that? Pity. Tell me about how in the world you came to be sat in front of me after having climbed the stairs and defeating the brotherhood, for I feel this is a story worth hearing." And, after couple of false starts Reg told the man his tale, the journey of his adventure and the challenges that he had over come. The friends he'd found, the friends he'd lost, the battle against the Brotherhood and the treasure that waited for him. The tale interested the man a great deal, and after some time he sat down with Reg.

"You have come far oh traveller of the world. This Tramp interests me a great deal. His story is, or rather was, more closely linked with your own than perhaps you know." Gorgain pondered a moment.

"Well, given I have told you my story, it would seem fitting that you should return the compliment," Reg responded, turning his head with a his ears ready to listen.

"The tramp was a cursed man, forced to live in Jidah under the rule of the Lord Mourdath. Unspeakable things happened to those who stayed in that world, terrible tortures I can't describe. Mourdath was a most terrible person, and he spent large portions of his time devising ways of inflicting pain on his victims. He created the Lestigona from the burnt flesh of more fortunate beings and gave the creature a malice unrivalled by any. The Lestigona was his most prized and most feared toy, eating the insides of its prey and leaving an empty corpse walking in its place." The man reflected for a moment before continuing. "It was only after a particular arrival in Jidah that things changed. A man cursed by a witch on your world was sent to Jidah, to be another play-thing for Mourdath. The Lestigona was unleashed on him, but this man was both fearless and stronger than any other ever to come in to Jidah. He caught the Lestigona by the throat and threw it through the dimensional wall that separate our worlds. The tramp and many others managed to escape at that time. This man though, he did not escape, nor did he try. He was not scared of this place or Mourdath. No, this man was quite unlike others from your world. Those that did escape however were tracked by the creature, for though it was lost of it's land it could smell Jidah on the skin of the escapists, and nothing could rid that smell. That is how Tramp knew the way to these places, that is also how the Lestigona found him, eventually." The man paused and stroked his long beard. Reg said nothing while the man reflected. "My name is Gorgain, I am the keeper of the realm. If you were in any doubt as to your whereabouts let me put it to rest. You are in the Kingdom of Letinah, the world between worlds, and I am the last of those who dwell here. The Brotherhood have lost their sanity it would seem, and I will join you in your quest for your treasure should you like my assistance. I ask only one question, please tell me—did you walk on the grass?"

"No," Reg said, "I did not."

"Good,"said Gorgain, "It took me ages to get it looking that nice." The host led his guest through the park, talking to him about the history of Jidah, of Letinah, the Brotherhood, Mourdath and the Lestigona. He talked and talked as they carried themselves many a mile to the edge of the park. Reg passed a glance up to Noah who sang a little birdsong, which made him smile. He felt much better about things again, he had Gorgain to guide him, Noah to keep him happy, and of course his trusty map, which had certainly led him on the exact path he drew, but through secret stairways, the depths of hell, portals to strange places and lots of other encounters he certainly hadn't anticipated. With a click of his fingers, Gorgain took them casually through a flash from nowhere back into the city Reg had left. The smell of pollution familiarised itself with Reg's senses once again, the grey, smoggy clouds loomed as ever and the traffic made an awful noise in the city rush hour. It always seemed to be rush hour, such is city living in the world where Reg resides.

"Which way?" Gorgain asked.

"What? I thought you knew the way?" said Reg a little surprised.

"I know the way in your world no better than you know the way in mine." Gorgain walked with a broad smile across his face. Reg found his map again and looked closely at the brown smudge of crayon mess.

Chapter 8
The Rookie Returns

It was a walk to the motorway they needed to cross, but that was very near the end of their journey. So it was then, and Gorgain, Reg and Noah were in fine spirits, singing songs and telling anecdotes to one another as they walked. There were tramps asking for money but they were not undead, Reg disbanded a few hoodies up to no good, Noah muted on an angry driver, Gorgain casually sent naughty children into different dimensions. All was going well, and they got to the far end of the city within an hour. When they arrived, they found the motorway had a tail-back for as far as the eye can see. At first Reg despaired, but Gorgain pointed out to him that if cars weren't moving at all, there was little or no risk of being hit by one, to which Reg and Noah both agreed.

So they started across the road, which was not such a hard task as the traffic was still, as indeed it never seems to be. That was until they heard a voice, familiar to Reg, just behind them.

"Oi! You! Stop right now!" Of course, it was our charming young police officer. He stepped out of his car, and this time he didn't care that it was left in the middle of the road, this time he was determined to catch his fugitive. Reg told his companions to fly like the wind and without question they did, quite literally in Noah's case. Gorgain leapt over the bonnets of several cars, dived over the barriers and did a double twist with a pike before his convincing landing which would've scored a perfect 10 in any competition. Noah landed himself on Gorgain's shoulder. Then they looked back over to see Reg slowly struggling to get past each car in turn, and the PC was only just behind him. Gorgain couldn't help but wonder how this man had managed to better any opponent, he was so slow! Despite the rigid determination on his face he would clearly struggle to win a race against a disabled tortoise. But, he had defeated all that had stood before him, and this commanded respect. So, Gorgain leapt back over the barrier, skipped passed the cars, grabbed Reg round the waist and took him to the other side, with the policeman at his heels. However, Gorgain's actions were not at all welcomed by Reg who struggled and wriggled all the way.

"Get your hands off me you charlatan," he cried, "I am not some child or toy you can pick up and throw around!" Gorgain put him back on his feet as soon as they were over the barrier. Reg, seething with anger, brushed himself down and straightened out his clothes before walking over to Gorgain, looking him in the eye, and slapping his face with all his might. Truly he was most upset, but Gorgain didn't really feel it as Reg, as we all know, isn't a terribly hard hitter. Despite this Gorgain thought it would be prudent to at least pretend the blow hurt him a little, he was in Reg's service and had no desire to offend him further. Reg raised a finger and was clearly about to give him a stern telling off when the Policeman came crashing over the barrier landing in a heap. Reg turned his head, though his finger remained under Gorgain's nose. The policeman picked himself up and dusted himself down, got his bearings and then turned his attention to Reg.

"You!" he said said in a guttural tone, clearly angry. Walking towards Reg menacingly with a face of thunder, the PC slipped on the damp grass, to which Reg and Gorgain couldn't help but snigger. The PC got back up, his uniform now stained green and with a large damp patch.

"Excuse me officer," Reg said cheekily. "Does your head go all the way to the top of that helmet?" Reg laughed to himself, joined by a large slap on the back from Gorgain who clearly thought the old joke quite hilarious. Even Noah gave a little chirp! But it just served to make the officer angrier still, and he walked slowly forward, reaching for his baton with a serious look of intent in his eyes.

"You are under arrest," the policeman said through gritted teeth. Reg and his friends laughed at him again, turned their backs and headed towards the lake, now well in sight and no more than a couple of miles walk. The officer roared to the skies before running up behind the group. "You will respect the law!" he screamed at the top of his lungs. "You are all coming with me!" Gorgain, not quite as well accustomed to the man as Reg, decided to approach him.

"You seem annoyed, what is that troubles you so much?" Gorgain spoke calmly and was really very friendly.

"This man is a fugitive. I have a warrant for his arrest and he'll not make a fool of me again!" Still seething the policeman looked as though he was at breaking point, clearly very stressed.

"What is your name lad?" Asked Gorgain.

"PC Dickens."

"Your first name?"

"Andy." Gorgain was calming him a little, but it was on a knife edge.

"Andy, you seem very angry. Surely Reg has not wronged you so badly?" Well, PC Dickens told him the whole story. This brought a smile to Gorgain's face on more than one occasion. "I think there's more than you're letting on," Gorgain said when Andy had finished. To which, the young policeman's face dropped, his lip started to tremble and his eyes welled up before he fell to his knees and cried like a new born baby as he blubbered his lamentable tail of how he was trampled on, bullied and generally looked down upon by the other bobbies at the station. Gorgain put a consoling arm round his shoulder and spoke warmly about sticking it to the man. Andy, in between the howling and blubbering agreed wholeheartedly. Then Reg came and stood over them.

"Would you like to join us on my quest?" Reg asked. Andy looked up at him. The sun was beginning to set and PC Dickens saw the eclipsed view of a wind-swept old man wearing his tri-cornered hat with a cutlass at his side.

"You're mad!" said Andy in confusion.

"No, he is not mad. We will find treasure on the island in the middle of the lake. Come, you look like a good man in need of good companions," Gorgain said, and he smiled so broadly and peacefully that when Reg offered Andy his hand, PC Dickens could not help but accept the proposal. He got up, threw down his badge and wiped his tears with the palm of his hand, leaving a brown mud-stain across the top of his cheek.

3 now became 4, and with the island in sight, the quartet walked off into the last phase of their adventure, all that remained was to collect the treasure that was destined for Reg. The sun started to set for the night as the next hour passed and the group decided to set up camp. Reg felt completely out of synch with his world and was most surprised when Andy told him that he'd escaped with Tramp only that morning, it felt considerably longer. A dozen transatlantic flights wouldn't account for the jet-lag he felt from dotting between worlds where it was either always night or always day, but as the night seized the remaining daylight, Reg's head rested on the earth and sleep took him seconds later. Gorgain put his cloak over him to make him comfortable. "Sleep my friend," whispered the Keeper of the realm gently, "destiny awaits you in the morning."

The following morning the group woke early from their slumber. The morning dew still covered the grass which reminded Reg and Andy of their first encounter in picnic area almost a week ago. One week. It seemed considerably longer to Reg, he felt like his life in that home back in, wherever it was, was in another reality all together. And now, alternate realities was something Reg actually had some knowledge about. He looked round at his crew—a wizard from the land of Jidah, a law enforcement officer, a wagtail who could understand English and him, an old man. Not a particularly daunting bunch he conceded, but the hard work was all done and all that remained was to take the final stroll down the lake, get over the water some how and wade ashore to claim his prize. Their prize. No, his prize. Maybe he'd throw them a bone or two, depending on if they earned it.

So, all packed, they started their walk. The hum of the motorway was the only distraction to what was really quite beautiful rural countryside. They were starting to get quite close as a group and they told stories as the lake before them got larger. It turned out Andy had a remarkable talent in dance, and actually had been in the English National Ballet before a minor injury led to him becoming a policeman. The other officers called him Sandy when they found out, and from then on it was impossible for him to win their respect. Even during pursuit of a villain, he would be running as fast as he could only to look back and see the others all skipping and laughing at him, slapping each others backs. More fool them Gorgain told him, jealousy was not a terribly becoming trait. Reg however was more or less convinced that Andy was a woofter, and kept his thoughts to himself. Gorgain told more of Jidah, much to Andy's bemusement, and performed levitation for his companions on more than one occasion. The three men got along very well all considered, and Noah sang song after song to keep spirits high.

It took longer than it felt, but by late morning they looked out across a vast lake at the small island in the centre. The island itself was little more than 40 feet across, and had a solitary tree in the centre, losing the last of it's leaves in the autumnal breeze. Reg cast his eyes over the stricken debris of rotting boats and wood that once carried men to and from the small island. There was no obvious way over; Reg was not much of a swimmer and had no real skill for wood craft. Of course the answer should have been relatively simple—Gorgain would use his powers to float the company across the lake. However, he found that his powers had no ability to lift over the water. This was, the party all agreed, most inconvenient; but Gorgain pointed out it is hard to know what skills you will retain during inter-dimensional travel, so in actual fact that he was able to use levitation at all was somewhat fortunate.

"Are you sure this is Nusketh?" Andy asked.

"Well," Reg poured over the map which by now was little more than one large smudge of colours, "Yes, this is definitely it. Damned fool," this time talking to himself, "Why on earth didn't I bring my armbands? Blast!"

The group sat down to ponder the problem. They must have been sat for an hour or more in relative silence, no-one offering much other than a series of half started sentences and umming and arring. This was until Reg suddenly stood up and walked to the water's edge.

"Pirates of Somerset!!! Hear me now! It is I, Reg, the last in your blood line! I have come for the treasure!" Reg's shouting was so fierce you might have thought his throat would not hold. The echoes of his call travelled across the lake unanswered. Reg then fell to his knees, defeated. He hung his head and closed his eyes, for he believed the treasure was no more than 1 mile from his grasp. A hush fell over them. At first it was just the sound of the voices that fell quiet, but then what little wind there was also dropped. The lake's water stopped moving all together. Gorgain tried to ask if anyone understood what was happening but he was unable to hear even the sound of his own voice.

Silence is an interesting subject. It is under normal circumstances impossible for a human to experience complete silence. When all noise has been removed, when nothing stirs at all, your hearing becomes more finely tuned to the small sounds that still occur, until eventually the only sound you can hear is your own blood being pumped around your body. When you cease to hear that, you cease to exist. Which is why the group of people that stood by the lake on that day felt particularly uneasy, for they could hear nothing; not the sound of their voices nor the blood through their veins. The incredible discomfort lasted only a few seconds but they were seconds that lasted an age, seconds in which all the questions you you've ever had could be answered twice over. And then the silence broke.

Chapter 9
Meet the In-Laws

Up out the the lake, from the deep fathoms of water between them and the island of Nusketh, a ship exploded into view sending spray for half a mile in every direction. A galleon that looked like it dated from the early 19th century (with Asda carrier bags and shopping trolleys and various other modern artifacts of the underwater world draped over it from hull to stern) now stood before them, rugged as Reg himself. Holes lined the port side of the ship that drained water by the gallon, and on deck a crew of quite bedraggled chaps looked towards the shore.

"Aargh!" called a pirate whilst shaking his cutlass above his head, seemingly at Reg. Reg's companions looked open-mouthed at the vessel, then at Reg, then back at the vessel. Reg in turned looked at them, before raising his own cutlass above his head and replying with the same, finely tuned "Arrharr!."

"Um, do you think that kind of behaviour wise?" Asked Andy who, though becoming more accustomed to the frankly ridiculous, was still white as a sheet from what had just happened.

"Why, he was just saying hello old boy," Reg said with a queer smile on his face. Then he turned back to look once more at the ship, which had a boat being lowered down the side. Two younger men clambered down the side of the ship and started rowing towards the shore. Reg and his companions looked on with a cross between excitement and amazement as the figures grew closer. The two of them were talking under their breath but no-one could hear what was being said. Undertones mixed with uncomfortable glances as they briefly looked at Reg and his company and then immediately averted their gaze as soon as they made eye-contact. The whole thing was, even with what came before it, just a bit weird.

Eventually they got to the shore, got out of the boat and stood before Reg. They nudged each other at first, and one muttered "No, you do it," to the other. A very uncomfortable disagreement ensued, before the scrawnier of the two (they were both more than a bit bedraggled but the elected chap was less than presentable) walked forward and engaged Reg with his eyes fixed firmly on his feet.

"Greeting, o…man o-o-of the shores of…where ever you're from…our es-t-teemed captain…err Grogbottom…challenges you to…um…a duel." His head was kept low throughout and he shifted his eyes back at his friend who's eyes were also set at the floor. The other lad caught his sight and offered the most apathetic of shrugs, before the speaker continued "We w-w-ait your response." Reg meanwhile was hardly able to keep the smile from his face and he looked round to his companions for their reactions. They in turn were still left somewhat surprised at the ship coming out of the water. Perhaps Gorgain less so, who was thoroughly enjoying this remarkable adventure. Before any of them had actually said a word, Reg turned back to the young scamps.

"With pleasure, I accept your captain's challenge." A twinkle in his eye and a strange smirk across his face, Reg walked towards the boys whilst looking at his friends who remained on the shore. Hand on his sword, he boarded the small boat calmly while the two lads pushed it out and then clambered on and manned the oars.

As they crossed, the creaking of the boat was the only sound to be heard. The pair who rowed kept their eyes on their feet, but Reg paid no heed. He looked across the water at the park benches, shopping trolleys, general litter and such like surrounding his ocean of destiny. He offered no conversation and sought none either, just patiently he waited, anticipating the moment; his moment, his final destination.

The boat reached the port side of the ship and a rope was thrown over to haul them aboard. Reg took the rope and started to clamber up the side. Of course, Reg not being a natural athlete, this activity was not a particularly successful activity. In fact, it took several attempts to get on to the rope at all, more than once did fall back into the boat in a heap.

This was of course all pretty awful and various shapes of pirates started laughing behind their hands in guttural tones not dissimilar to that of a spluttering motorcycle. But eventually, after a few falls, a couple of bumps and some minor damage to the side of the ship, Reg heaved himself over top and fell like a sack of potatoes onto the deck. A little shaken by the experience, it's already established after all that exercise is not a hobby of our hero's, Reg took a few seconds panting on the slightly splintered wooden surface regaining his breath. When he did though, and when the cloud lifted from his eyes, he saw before him the formidable size 14 boot of the infamous Captain Grogbottom.

Reg looked up at the grotesque face of the Captain, and he found a pair of wild looking eyes staring back at him. They studied each other for a time, Reg's shirt was a little torn in places and threaded on the sleeves. His trousers were muddy and dirty, his pots and pans and satchel were gone altogether, truth be told Reg looked pretty scruffy. But the man stood before him, he bore a stomach that could home several barrels of grog, clothed only in tattoos and body hair. His trousers were rags from the knee down, and his impressive (if not a little odd) fine size 14 black boots came up just past his ankles. His eyes were crinkled, his face heavily lined and a queer look of bewilderment and surprise surpassed his suggestion of authority. His head was completely bald, and his beard came down as far as his chest. It was black but streaked with grey, and when he opened his mouth the teeth he bore were almost totally brown and black.

"Ya battled on this world and the next?" said the deep gravely tone of Grogbottom.

"That I have," Reg answered.

"Aargh, I bet ya have. Ya read the omen as well I suppose?"

"Yes," Reg answered.

"What was it just out of interest?"

"Frankie's has been shut for 23 years." A moment of confused silence fell then, and Grogbottom looked at his first mate a little unsure, and the first mate shrugged back at him.

"Aargh, I see." This was all Grogbottom said to that. "And what of the curse? Do ya know of the curse?"

"Curse? No, I'm afraid I don't know about any curse. It's treasure that I want." Reg spoke almost casually but the mention of treasure sent the pirates into a frenzied attack of laughter. Two lads laughed so hard they actually fell off the rigging.

"I'm sorry," Grogbottom said, fighting the laughter, "but I did for one second think you said you wanted treasure!"

"What else will you give me as a prize for defeating you?" This remark resulted in a deep intake of breath from the crew followed by "oohs" to their captain. He in turn laughed again, but a much slower, deeper laugh this time.

"We aven't got no treasure," Grogbottom had his eyes fixed on Reg's as he spoke, "Can I interest you in anythin' else?" Grogbottom's crew were quickly becoming something of a panto audience as they cheered everything their captain said and mocked Reg in one way or another. Reg in turn stood resolute, allowing his eyes to be met by Grogbottom' s fierce gaze.

"I shall assume control of your vessel and your crew." About that time, the expression "laughing yourself to death" had a pretty significant meaning, as young Nodder, a deck hand who couldn't swim, cried so hard at these words that he actually fell overboard. His frantic thrashing in the water lasted a minute or so, and the crew all looked over at him as he struggled, before he eventually sank like a cannonball. The pirates hushed for a minute or so, then Grogbottom addressed his crew.

"'E's been trapped 'ere waiting for a curse to break so 'e can live again, and when it's broken 'e dies o' laughter! That's, err, what d'ya call it? Men?" His men rarely disappoint, but on subjects of grammar they often struggled. They were in fact a sea of blank faces. Until one man had a sudden eureka moment, and started waving his hand in the air.

"I know sir, I know! It's, um, err, it's colonic?" Everyone rubbished, shouting at him calling him an idiot. "Plutonic?" More rubbishing, a little laughter. "Symphonic?" Just laughter.

"Ironic," shouted out Reg, surprising himself as much as anyone else. Grogbottom looked round at him, as did everyone else. Still smiling though, the captain looked upwards and stroked his beard.

"Aye, that's the one. Where were we?"

"Duelling."

"Ah yes, the dual. You want me ship if ya win, I remember now. But what makes ya think me boys 'ere will be interested in followin' a scruffy lookin' thing like ya self?" More panto noises from the crew.

"I believe I am a descendant of yours." More laughter, more jeering. Grogbottom included.

"Ya look nothin' like me!" The pirate then thought for a few minutes. "Ya did however break me curse, and that had to be done by me own blood," the crew started to quieten down at that point. "Could be possible," he mused further. "Ok, agreed." Grogbottom signalled to one of his men who threw him a cutlass, and he advanced quickly on Reg.

"But what do you want if you win?" Reg said, retreating slightly.

"Don't care!" said Grogbottom, and then with his eyes closed, he started wildly swinging his blade, edging forward a little at a time. Reg was more used to a traditional en garde and couldn't see how he would fight such a manic technique, if you could even call it that. His own sword was barely drawn when Grogbottom's first blow came thundering down on his shaky defence, and Reg was knocked to the floor by the power of the attack. Quickly he rolled over, and a good thing to as that same blade of Grogbottom's buried itself in the deck where Reg's head had been moments before. Reg continued to roll and if Grogbottom had at any point the sense to actually open his eyes he would surely have slew his man in seconds. But open them he did not, and through luck and bad timing on Grogbottom's part, Reg continued to roll about 8 inches in front of the cutlass that continued to fall over and over again next to his head. This stopped abruptly however when Grogbottom swung too hard a got it stuck in the wood. Reg got to his feet and started to run away, though as we all know Reg isn't a man for speed. He'd got only a few yards when a cutlass came flying past his head and lost itself inside one of Grogbottom's crew. This served to upset the captain greatly, and in the fit of rage he had become so famous for all those years ago he picked up the nearest thing he could find, which was Berrin the cabin boy, and threw him with all his might at Reg. He didn't hit Reg though, for it there's three things in the world Grogbottom's no good with, it's patience, manners and accuracy. Poor young Berrin found himself flying through the air before clipping his leg against the hull and falling towards the water, bumping off the ship on the way down. This continued for a time then, with Reg dodging various members of the crew who suffered anything from broken bones to flying over the side.

And as it is to continue for some time, allow me to explain why they are fighting, for it is not to be spoken of by either Reg or Grogbottom. Grogbottom and his men waved their cutlasses in the air and made guttural shouting noises to Reg on the shore, or so he thought. It was actually just made towards them generally, but as it was Reg that carried the cutlass it was he that received the address. The gesture they made from the ship was not them simply being friendly, it was a warning, which Reg had unfortunately rebuked by mimicking their actions. So upset was Grogbottom that he decided to challenge Reg at that time. While he was coming to the ship in the little rowing boat, it occurred to Grogbottom that he no longer seemed to be in the cursed land of Jidah. However, as his time there was not particularly distressing, he did not dwell on the subject. Until that is, he remembered that there were some conditions or other as to why he had been able to come back. Unfortunately, it wasn't of any great interest to him thereafter and the thought of duelling was far too tempting. Reg had no idea why he was duelling, but didn't like to ask for fear of coming across weak. So that's that.

Now, as Reg and Grogbottom at this point were still locked in much the same activities as they were when we left them, let us briefly return to the shore with Andy, Gorgain and Noah. Andy was sat down on the bed of sand, mud and shingle, throwing pebbles towards the water. Gorgain stood at his side looking out to the ship, and Noah was picking worms out of the ground.

"What do you suppose is going on?" Gorgain queried. Andy looked up at him.

"Well," Andy said pulling himself to his feet. He brushed the dirt from his hands and observed the ship himself. "Err, it would appear Reg is running for his life from a man who is throwing other men at him." The observation was accurate enough, and he looked at Gorgain for a reaction.

"Yes, that appears to be right." That was all he offered.

"I thought we just had to get some treasure from the little island over there, what the hell is going on?"

"Truth be told I don't know. I might go back to Letinah, I miss my lawn."

"How long have you been away?"

"Such lovely grass it is, neat and trim. That's how grass should look you know." Gorgain looked at Andy, made a strange "Blah" sound, and then vanished. Andy looked at Noah who was flicking his head to get the worm down his gullet.

"Mad, the whole thing's mad!" said Andy to the small bird.

"You're mad," said Noah, and after grabbing another worm he flew off to the little island, apparently satisfied his mission was complete. Which left Andy on his own. He contemplated a talking bird, a vanishing man, a pirate ship appearing from nowhere and a crazy pensioner. Too much, it was too much. Andy turned his round from the water and walked back the way he came. He did look back at the boat, long enough shake his head and scratch his temple, and then he carried on walking. He didn't go back to the police service.

Anyway, Reg was trying to stay alive in his "dual" with Grogbottom, and as things were about to take a change significant enough as to be worth telling, we should return to the ship. Reg was extremely tired from all his running, and Grogbottom was a little tired himself from all his pirate throwing, and so more or less at the same time, they sat down for a rest. Reg on port side and Grogbottom on the starboard. The members of the crew who had not been thrown brought some foul tasting rum to their captain, and those who had been thrown writhed about in agony. Reg sat panting, his cutlass at his side, and his eyes were once again met by his opposite number.

"Will ya take a drink master Reg?" said Grogbottom who himself was panting a little.

"Certainly," Reg said as he tried to slow his breathing. A bottle of grog was rolled across the deck from the captain's hand to Reg's feet. He took out the stopper and took a big swig. Reg made a contented sound before saying something under his breath.

"What was that ya said man?" growled the captain.

"I said it was most refreshing," Reg said as he drank again.

"Come again?" Grogbottom leaned forward.

"Very nice," Reg called out. Grogbottom looked hard at him, studying his face. Then he smiled, a smile that had not surfaced in a long time. For this smile was not the smile of a successful pillage, nor was it the smile of waking up on a bed of treasure. It was a smile that you can only have when you have related to someone or something, a common interest, a shared opinion, a private joke. A way of letting someone know you understand them, and such an event had not become of Grogbottom since he was still known as Pipkins. He turned his eyes to the deck as he was unable to conceal this face any other way.

"Aye, that it is," he said. Then he looked back up at Reg and actually let out the most heart felt laugh he had ever had. "It be me favourite drink, so it does!"

"I can see why," said Reg who didn't quite follow all this so well as he was unaware of Grogbottom's personal history, but he was very happy to see the man apparently warming to him. And warming he was, unified by a mutual affection for foul-tasting liquor. Grogbottom was now laughing loudly, no holding back, no charade, just loud, proud laughter. And then he stood up. "Boggins!" he shouted out, "Boggins come 'ere right now!" And a man came over to receive a cutlass through his torso and then found himself falling overboard, took a couple of deep breathes of water and fell to darkness. Grogbottom was still laughing, slapping his thy with a fine gusto. "Reg me man, I seem to o' lost me first mate, would ya like the job?" Reg felt that same smile invade his face just like it had Grogbottom's, the laughter followed, and he pulled himself to his feet. The two men laughed as they walked towards one another, and when they met they shook hands warmly. This was followed by the first embrace either man had had since their respective childhoods.

"Behold me brother, ya new first mate, REG! Reg, a pirate, like us, among his new family! Aargh!" Grogbottom held up Reg's hand triumphantly as he cheered that wonderful pirate cheer, and those of his crew who were able to do so cheered as well, and those struggling on the deck gave a heavy groan as best they could. And Reg, Reg felt a warmth within himself he could not describe. A feeling of destiny, of euphoria, of victory, all the most incredible emotions a man is capable of feeling Reg went through right then.

This was just about the end of the adventure, there are only three more things to tell. One is that Reg was taken ashore to Nusketh, a small patch of wasteland the borough council of the area neglected, where he and Grogbottom dug out a treasure chest as big as a wardrobe, full of the most wonderful treasure, stones and metals that represent the reason people take to piracy in the first place.

The second is that the lake that homed Nusketh was from then on the most feared body of water in the world, and Grogbottom and Reg enjoyed the spoils of extremely bad behaviour for a long time to come.

The final thing is that a year later, in a theatre of no particular name, in a town of no particular significance, an amateur dance society performed a work of no notable worth. The lead belonged a chap who once used to chase criminals. He'd never been happier.